Frederic Spencer

# La vie de sainte Marguerite. An Anglo-Norman version of the XIIIth century.

Now first edited from the unique manuscript in the University Library of

Cambridge, and accompanied by an introduction, together with critical and

explanatory notes, and a br

Frederic Spencer

**La vie de sainte Marguerite. An Anglo-Norman version of the XIIIth century.**
*Now first edited from the unique manuscript in the University Library of Cambridge, and accompanied by an introduction, together with critical and explanatory notes, and a br*

ISBN/EAN: 9783741183829

Manufactured in Europe, USA, Canada, Australia, Japa

Cover: Foto ©Andreas Hilbeck / pixelio.de

Manufactured and distributed by brebook publishing software (www.brebook.com)

Frederic Spencer

**La vie de sainte Marguerite. An Anglo-Norman version of the XIIIth century.**

# La Vie

de

# Sainte Marguerite.

## An Anglo-Norman Version of the XIII th Century.

Now first edited from the unique Manuscript in the University
Library of Cambridge, and accompanied by an Introduction,
together with critical and explanatory Notes, and a brief
account of the Development of the Margaret Legend

by

## Frederic Spencer

Assistant-master in the Leys School, Cambridge.

# A Dissertation

for

the Degree of Doctor in Philosophy in the University
of Leipsic.

# The Cambridge MS. Ee VI. XI.

This version of the legend, which is now edited for the first time, is not found elsewhere. The opening and concluding verses have been published by Mr. Paul Meyer in Romania (XV, 268). I cannot do better than quote his description of the Manuscript which contains the same.

"Ce MS. se compose de deux morceaux distincts reliés ensemble

1° Cahiers 1 et 2 (feuillets 1—15). Vie de Sainte Marguerite et Purgatoire. Le premier cahier (ff. 1—8) est complet en huit feuillets, le second n'en a que sept, le huitième, qui était probablement blanc, ayant été coupé. L'écriture paraît être de la seconde moitié du XIIIᵉ Siècle: les dimensions du parchemin sont 176ᵐᵐ sur 120ᵐᵐ.

2° Cahiers 3 à 5 (22 feuillets). Fables de Marie de France; l'écriture est plus ancienne que celle des deux cahiers précédents. Je l'attribuerais à la première moitié du XIIIᵉ Siècle. Hauteur des feuillets 176ᵐᵐ, largeur 132ᵐᵐ."

The "Vie de Sainte Marguerite" is a rhymed version in alexandrine lines arranged in strophes of varying length. The most superficial examination suffices to detect the Anglo-norman origin of the version in its present form.

Indeed, in view of certain passages, it seems questionable whether the last copyist had any but a most rudimentary knowledge of the French Language (cf. e. g. vv. 48, 87, 176, 242, 252, 387 &c.). Some passages point more conclusively to ignorance of the written, than of the spoken language (e. g. me plays 132; le chevus 194 &c.).

Among the most striking evidences of the Anglonorman origin of the text in its present form the following may be instanced.

A large number of lines are either too long or too short, varying between 8 and 14 syllables (cf. vv. 107, 207 &c.). In cases where it is possible to establish the original text such errors are found to be not alone due to the carelessness of copyists. The French language had a distinct and more rapid development on English soil, and an Anglonorman was not always sure of the number of syllables to be attributed to a given word.

Further: The declension system is in a stage of complete corruption. It is not necessary to quote from the abounding instances of this phenomenon.

Distinctions of Grammatical Gender are more or less effaced, owing to the influence of the English vernacular. Our poem affords many instances of this neglect of gender-distinctions. We find e. g. un clarte 204 (cf. Destruction de Rome le toen bountee) and le alme 275; as well as numerous cases of confusion between the masculine and feminine forms of other inflected parts of speech (e. g. le haist 37, le ust 40). In fact all the varied inflections of the article, as well as of possessive and demonstrative pronouns are constantly confused with one another, or otherwise maltreated (e. g. me dolurs 130, me plays 132, le chevus 194 &c.).

Another salient point is the constant neglect of the caesura, instances of which are frequent on every page. It will be seen later that I do not refer this state of metrical chaos to the original old French form of this version.

In many words we find the English w representing the Romance v (e. g. awant 86, dewaunt 92, wous 157); and the substitution of y for i without any guiding principle is of constant occurrence (e. g. crei, crey: murir, muryr: ki, ky &c.).

**My** is found instead of **mon**, and the respective functions of **ke** and **ki** are continually interchanged.

The sibilants **s** and **z** are also frequently interchanged without any fixed principle.

The orthography of the manuscript could not indeed be worse than it is, without becoming at the same time unintelligible. The same word is often spelt in a variety of ways. So **puse** 91, **puisse** 280, **pusse** 107, **pousse** 259; so also **puis** 225, **pois** 227 (**puse**(!) 228): cf. **seignur, seinur, senniur, seingor, sengor; aime, arme** &c.

The preference of the orthography **u** for, **o** (Lat. ō, ŭ) is seen in **aure** 185, 204, but we also find the alternative, as in **trover**. The same sound is also represented by the orthography **ou**, (**aoure** 110: so 180, 336).

We find again **o** for **ue** (Lat. ŏ) as in **pople** 141.

Further the sounds **ai ei** are not distinct, and are both indifferently represented by **e**. We have accordingly **fere** by the side of **faire**; **meintenant** and **mentenir**. So **de** stands for **dei** in 124; cf. **arder** 280 and again **veintre** (vaincre) 91.

Common also is the orthography **e** for **ie**. So **pecche** 343, **targer** 281, **sacez** and **sachez** for saciez &c. Further we find **chier** 119, **chief** 373 &c., which show that the open and close **e** were not distinguished, and, when confounded, might assume the orthography **ie**; **ei** is also written for **e** (as in **torneir** 356). Rhymes of **-ier** with **-er** exist, and will be discussed later.

The anglonorman orthography **aun-** for **an-** before a consonant is exemplified in **auncessor** 98. Remark also the fluctuating orthography **oi ei** (108—112).

Very common is the slurring of **e** mute, not only after vowels, but also after consonants and combinations of consonants — and this not only in groups consisting of a mute and liquid. Examples abound. Thus a **hunte** 282, **turbes** 269, **promesse** 120 &c.

Indeed so complete has this neglect of the **e** mute become that our copyist often omits it at the end of a word, e. g. **neie** 209 (cf. vv. 25 and 26 where another flexion is added in its place). He also adds it where it should not exist as **lapideez** 9, **parentee** 20, 67 &c.

The neglect of a mute **e** after a consonant at the end of a word does not occur in rhyme, but this redeeming feature is of course not to be placed to the credit of the copyist. As to the occurrence of **creatur (creature?)** 97, this will be noticed elsewhere.

The orthographies **lli, ngn** to represent the sounds $\bar{\text{l}}$ and ñ are worthy of notice (**ovellies** 58, **narillies** 170, **ingnelement** 320, **veingne** 300; cf. **saliir** 153).

The alternation of certain verbs between the conjugations in **-er** and **-ir** (also a sign of Anglonorman orgin) has been fully discussed in the note to v. 34. Cf. however **honeint** 386.

We have then a poem copied in the latter half of the XIII[th] Cy. by an Anglonorman or English scribe. It is evident from the first that this is not the original form of the text.

There are unfortunately no other texts by the aid of which we might arrive at the original with some degree of certainty, and, in the corrupt state of our Ms., any plausible conjectures can only be based on considerations of rhyme, metre, elision &c. The poem is written in verses of 12 syllables, which should have a caesura at the end of the 6th. The grouping of the verses into strophes of unequal length might induce one to hazard the supposition that the original text had been written in assonance, but had shared the same fate as other and more important works (such as St. Alexis, Chanson de Roland, and many Chansons de Gestes), assuming at the hands of unscrupulous time-servers another and corrupted form, in which rhymes were substituted for the earlier assonances. In the text as we have it there is not wanting internal evidence to render this hypothesis at least a plausible one. The strophe 87—91 affords the phenomena referred to. From the point of view of assonance there is no incorrectness in this strophe, whereas, on the other hand, it transgresses the laws of rhyme. The final vowels are derived either from Latin ō (nuns, felluns, perillius) or from ŭ (lus). The appearance of **respuns** (responsum) in such a laisse is not unusual (cf. Horning § 66 and Alexis p. 59 note 1). Remark here **awoglez** (353) in a strophe in **-er.**

I am not inclined to accept **pensenz** (7) as an original reading, at least in this assonance. Its acceptance would necessitate the hypothesis of a date earlier than other considerations warrant. Such an assonance is allowable in St. Leger, but no longer in St. Alexis (cf. St. Alexis p. 82). The strophes in **-ist** do not help materially towards any certain decision. It might be argued that several of the end-words should end in **it** (e. g. **finist** 42, **encontredist** 44), but, on the other hand, anglonorman poets often insert this s from analogy with other words in which its presence is legitimate. Assuming again that these endings were correctly written in a supposed earlier assonanced poem, they would have fulfilled all the requirements of assonance.

With regard to the strophe 87—91 it might be suggested that line 89 should follow 91, a change which would satisfy the requirements of rhyme, and not injure the sense of the passage. But the strophe 125—131 contains further material in favour of the hypothesis. Even here, however, line 131 might be placed after 128, but the construction would be strained, while the existing arrangement yields excellent sense.

In my note to line 74 I have suggested the reading **mult irez s'en alerent** for the sake of **amerent** 73, which would else remain unrhymed. These two lines however may well have been the first lines of a strophe in **-irent**, and may have read thus: ... **plus sa beaute a(d)mirent** ... **mult forment il s'en irent.** Burguy does not give **admirer,** but latinisms were frequent among anglonorman poets (cf. Vie de St. Grégoire Romania VIII, 203).

Leaving the question of assonance on one side, it is at least demonstrable that the rhymed version is of anglonorman origin. We find the usual confusion of rhymes in -er and -ier, though in very small numbers. We find thus aïder in a strophe in -er (v. 19). So aporter 291 in a strophe in -ier. Deneer in 335 might be read deveer. Cf. also vv. 277, 373. On the other hand we often find careful distinction, and grouping together of the endings in -ier. So 125—131 (cf. remarks on this strophe above), 162—165, 222—226 (which I have divided from the following rhymes in -er) and 255—259 (similarly divided from preceding rhymes in -er).

In 144 we find aver in a strophe in -er (Lat. āre) a phenomenon which does not occur before about 1200 (Suchier, Vie de St. Auban). Consentir (272) must also have been written consenter. For this agn. peculiarity see note on line 34.

The rhymes -ant, -ent are, for the eye, distinct: another characteristic of agn. verse. Some however in -ant are among those which have usurped the place of original forms in -ent (e. g. garant 85, remanant 378 &c). This subject is fully treated by Suchier, Reimpredigt p. 69 ss.

The occurrence of creatur in 97 is one of the most startling phenomena to be found in our text. To understand creator (creatorem) does not suit the spirit of Olibrius' speech, unless indeed we see in the tyrant's blasphemous utterances an element of intended irony. I am loath however to read creature (creatura) which would be inconsistent with the purity of the other rhymes in -or. Indeed such a reading, if established, would point to the very last stage of anglonorman deterioration, and would force us to a date hardly earlier than the copy which we possess. Suchier places the introduction of the rhymes ū: ō, ŭ between 1220 and 1250, and the neglect of a 'mute' e after a final consonant, in rhyme, still later (Vie de St. Auban). The mistake **creatur** for **traïtur** would not have been surprising even in the case of a more careful copyist (see note on this line). Again the original may have had **malfaitur** (cf. Garnier du Pont St. Max., Bartsch 259. 2).

The other rhymes of the poem present no phenomena of interest. In 62 **ancele** (ancilla) rhymes, as often, with words in **-ell-**. **Pounee** (of unknown derivation) rhymes with **ventree** in Apostr. au Corps 74 (Bartsch), and thus stands correctly in 27. Considerations of rhyme lead me to adopt **ge-ïr** as the reading of 78 (see note on this line): **gésir** gives **gire** (Burguy I, 345).

The strophe 199—202 perhaps requires mention. The rules as to the agreement of the past participle in reflexive verbs (**reclamer** 199) are somewhat lax in old French, especially in the anglonorman developments. We have thus an anomalous form in **torne**(e) 64.

**Esperitez** in 202 is not to be understood as **esperitee**, thus maltreated for the sake of rhyme. It may be regarded as having **esperitels** for its original form, which, in an assonanced laisse, would be perfectly correct. For identity of masc. and fem. forms in this adjective we have parallels in the "Sermons de St. Bernard". The neglect of agreement in the participle **levez** 372 is not an unusual phenomenon.

Thus the rhymed version of which Ee VI, XI. contains a copy is of anglonorman origin, and dates from a period not earlier than 1200. If **creatur** (97) is to be accepted as an authentic reading, representing Lat. **creatura**, the date must be fixed much later. It seems probable that the rhymed version is a 'remaniement' of an older assonanced version, for the determining of whose date materials are not forthcoming.

I have said little or nothing concerning the metre. The long dispute as to the construction of anglonorman verse, in which Suchier, Meyer, Paris, Vising have taken a prominent part, seems to have been settled once for all by the publi-

cation of "La Vie de S. Grégoire par Frère Augier" (Romania
XII, 145). It seems established that the Anglonorman poets
aimed at correct French versification, and that their errors
were due to ignorance or carelessness, not to any universal and
definite influence of another metrical system. For the majo-
rity of the errors we must consider copyists to be respon-
sible. I have suggested (pp. 31, 32) emendations reinstating
the alexandrine metre of the incorrect verses, endeavouring
to provide for the proper observance of rules concerning
the caesura. Most of the suggested emendations call for no
further knowledge than that of the most common omissions
and interpolations of anglonorman scribes, fully treated by
Suchier (Vie de St. Auban) and by Vising (Versification anglo-
normande).

# The Text.

(Cambridge Ee. VI. XI.)

I give the text here exactly as it stands in the manuscript. In two cases I have neglected a brachygraph which seems to be an error of the copyist, and which, in one case, undoubtedly is so. To these variations I have referred in the notes. It might have been well to omit the e after u where it is introduced merely to indicate the consonantal nature of the latter, but I shrank from the forms anjle &c. which consistency would then have demanded.

———

Puis ke Deus nostre sire de mort resucita,
Veant ses angleles a son pere monta,
Granz companies de seinz e de sentes y lessat,
E puis pur luy morrurent e yl les corrunat:
5   Del son celestre regne large pars lur dunat.

A icel tens diable aveient granz poetez,
Pur seinte Yglise prendre esteient si pensenz,
Quant il trovent nul hom qui seyt cristienez,
Si esteit pendu ou ars ou lapideez,
10   Ou destret de chivaus ou haut el vent croulez:
Mes cil ke n'en chaleit tant en ert honurez
Que en permanable glore en est corunez.

Seinurs des toz les autres vus lerai a conter,
Fors de une sule virge me covent parler.
15   Son seinur celestre tant pout toz jurs amer,
Onkes pur nul turment que l'em le sout duner,
Ne pur nule promesse ne wout de luy torner.
Trayez ca vers moy: pri vus de l'escoter,
Car vers son chier senniur vus pout ben aider.

20 Ceste pucele fu mult de haut parentee;
Si pere fu paiens de grant nobilitee,
Theodorus out nun, onkes ne cremout De,
Tuz ceus qui creeint en Deu out il en vilte,
Nule rien ne hait envers cristiente.

25 Margarete la gente out nun, de la contre ert nez,
Mult fu bele e curteysse, sage e honurez,
De co secle hait la mauveise pounee,
En luy a mis son quor e tote sa pensee,
A cel senniur s'est prise, jammes n'ert esgaree.
30 Dec ove les seinte virgens ert en cel honuree.

Senniurs ore vus dirum de ceste Deu amie
Sa vie e ses mors e cum ele fu nurie,
E cum Olibrius l'occist e par grant emvie,
E cum gloriusement ele finat sa vie,
35 E cum ele parvint a la Deu companie.

La bele Margarete pus ke ele fu nee
En une cite fu nurrie e commandee
Ke de Antioche fu unce liues messuree,
A une prude femme ki ele fu liveree.
40 Ele la norrist si ben cum si ele le ust portee,
Unkes pur nul engin ne pouit estre blamee.

Quant avint issi ke sa mere finist,
En emfern alad si cum le livere dist,
Maves hostel i trova sanz nul encontredist.
45 E la bone norrice Margarete norrist,
Ele l'amóut assez plus l'amast e igist.
Contre co k'ele l'amat e si pere le haist.
Bien fu de sa nurice: onc de luy ne partist
Des i ke Olibrius le provost le seisist.

50 Tant nurist la meschine ke ele pout aler,
E ke ele fu resonable e sage de parler.
Les passiuns de martirs oeit reconter,

E les uns oeit arder, les autres lapider,
Echorcher tuz vis ou pendre ou decoler.
55   A idunc commenzat en Deu sey a fermer,
Jammes ne departirat pur tote demembrer.

Co fu a cel tens que ele aveit quinze ans,
Les vellies gardout ove les autres enfanz,
Del chimin la chosist un mauveys tirant.

60   Un culvert a dist: ore vey une pucele,
Onkes al men escient ne veistes plu bele:
Alez demandez luy si ele fraunche ou ancele,
En quel deu ele creyt e comment l'um l'apele.

Li mestre felon s'en sunt d'ilec tornee,
65   A luy vindrent ensemble com lur fu commandee,
Si ele franche ou ancele co luy hunt demandee,
E de quel creance ele est e de quel parentee.

La gloriuse virgne lor respond bonement,
Car ele ert replenie de grant aseinement:
70   Crestiene sui franche: co respund vereiment.
En Deu le fiz Marie crei jo parfitement,
Qui regneyt sor toz jurs e ert parfitement.

Mes cum parole plus plus sa beaute amerent:
Quant il sa creance oient munt s'en irent:
75   D'ilokes s'en sunt tornez, demorrance ne firent,
Al provost l'on conte, de nent ne luy mentirent.

Arreement lur dist: fetes la moy venir.
Par toz se deus en iore il luy estoveit geyr,
Autrement le frad de male mort muryr.
80   Sanz demorance cil l'alerent sesyr.

Butint e decirent cil maves tirant,
E de diz e de fecz la wont contraliant.
Ne seit ke deit fere, anguisse ad grant;
Vers le ciel regarde la bele a son amant;

85 Ducement luy ad dist: mester ay de garant,
Beau pere meintenez moy des ore en awant.

Byeu sire gardez moy pur tes intime nuns,
Pere ne perdez m'alme ho ces maves felluns,
Autresi suy entre eus com owaillye entre lus.
90 Ottreez a faire au provost teus respuns
K'il ne me puse veintre par torment perillius.

A iceste paroles wint dewaunt le felon.
Il luy a demande son linghage e son nun,
E en quel deu ele creit die luy sanz tencun:
95 Cristiene suy franche: ce respond sanz tencun:
Si crey en Jhesu Crist e Margarete ay a nun.

Creys tu dunc Margarete en icel creatur
K'en la croiz occist mi auncessur?
Oil, fet Margarete, luy crei jo e aour.
100 Co lur torne onkore a mult grant deshonur,
En emfert le pulent sofrent grant dolur.

Si irez fu luy provost quant il l'oieit parler,
En un oscure chartre la commanda enserer,
De ke ele eit torment dont la puisse dampner.
105 En Antioche veit pur ses deus aurer,
Pur cristiens querre: de cel ne wount cesser,
K'il il ne pusse a hunte occire e grevement tormenter.

Quant il fu repeyre fist la venir a sey,
Dist luy: bele pucele aiez merci de tey,
110 Mes deus puanz aoure, e si crey en ma ley:
Grant avoyr te duray, co sachez par ma foy,
E a femme te prendray, e bien seras de moy.

Margarete respund sanz autre demorance:
Co seit Deus le men pere en ky ay esperance,
115 Ke a son os me garde co sachez sanz dotance,
Ke pur reyn que me diez ne perderay ma creance.

Coluy voil je amer e aurer e duter
Ke tote choses garde, cel e terre e mer,
E secle de secles ne lerad sun regner.
120 Pur nule promesse que facez ne voyl de luy torner,
A luy voil je mun cors e m'alme commander,
Ke ove les seintes virgnes me face reposer.
Pur nus deinad son cors a mort li sire deliverer,
E je pur luy murir ne de mie duter.

125 Tote nue la fit dewant luy despulier,
En l'eyr la fit suspendre e de verges trencher,
E ele commence son seinniur a prier:
Sire aidez moy que je en ay mester,
En vus ay m'esperance, pere ne me lessez,
130 Enclin ka ta oreillie, me dolurs me leschez
Ke cil ne me charnissent qui vers moy sunt si fer.

Le richies commenca a preier la meschine:
Beau pere envey a me plays medicine.
En dementers ke la virgne sa priere define
135 La mavesse metnee del luy batre ne fine.
Le sanc vermel li curt aval par la peistrine
Cum ewe de funteyne qui curt par grant ravine.

Olibrius co veit, si commenca a crier:
Bele purquey te les a hunte tormenter?
140 Crei Margarete, ne te les dampner.
Le pople qui l'esgardent ne finent de plurer
Pur le sanc que veient de son cors avaler.
En plurant li unt pris ducement a mostrer:
Bele kar en pensez de te merci aver,
145 Iirez est li provost, ne te lerat durer.

E vus conselier: Margarete dist lur:
Alez a vos osteus, n'ay soin de vostre plur:
Deus est mi aiders en ki je crei e aur.
E cum fere pucele tant eimet son seinnur,

2

150 De sey ne ad manee ne pite ne tendrur.
Vereiment est pleyne de spirital amur.

Li macecren adecertes ne finent de ferir,
Li sanc vermeyl en funt de tote pars saliir.
Li provost e li pople ne pount mes suffrir,
155 Lur oiz de lur meyns commencent a coverir.
Olibrius li dist ke l'eimed a hunir:
Si tu ne wous mes deus aurer e servir,
Tes os fray dejoindre e tes nerfs departyr.

Margarete respunt cum femme membree:
160 Culvert fel e hardi, si ma char est pelfree
M'alme ert en ciel hautement corunee.

Dolenz est li provost, n'i out que corucer,
Fet la en une chartre meintenant trebucher.
Cele n'eubliad mie son seinnur a prier,
165 E de la seynte croyz toit son cors a seinnier.

Este vus o uns draguns de la chartre sallieit,
Orible e ydus de leidde forme esteit:
Chevus de plusurs guise, russe barbe aveit,
Ses denz erent ferines sez ouz luisanz dreit,
170 De buche e de narillies fu e flamme isseit,
Un serpent de maleire sor le col li seeit,
Un espee ardante en sa meyn teneit.

En la chartre estuit, fortment prist a siflyr,
N'i out tant oschur liu ou l'um ne veit ja cler.
175 Tel pour oust la virgne quant issi l'ot demener,
Quan vis pout onkes sor ses pez ester.
A oresuns se torne, oec ne wout oblier,
Cum sule orfanine Deu prist a reclamer.
Pri li ke li let au dragun devurer.

180 En dementers que ele oure e li dragun la sesist,
Si cum livere dist vive la transglutist.

Ne pout sofrir la croiz dont ele sa garnist,
Lui draguns en deu pars meintenant defendist:
Seinne e save e halegree meintenant s'en issist.

185  Del dragum ke ele oust vencu grant joie demenat.
Aj es un autre diable a son fenestre estat,
De mult leid figure, home neir resemblat:
Les menys e le cheffuz ensemble liez ad.
Quant le veit la pucele mult grant pour en ad,
190  Vers Dampnedeu se torne, sun nun glorifiat.
Sa oreysun ad feite, Deus ottreez l'at.
Dementers ke la virgne sun sengor priat,
Li adversers s'aprimat, par la meyn seisi l'at.

Ele fu de Deu soure, par le chevus li prist,
195  Par Deu virtu le tret que a terre le mist,
E puis sun destre pe sor le col li assist.
Alez vus ent de moy: la seinte pucele li dist:
O malingnes esperiz, tute destruit Jhesu Crist.

A la beste pudlente de enfern m'est reclamez:
200  Cesse de ma persone, tot te confunde Deus.
En moy ni avera tu rien cheteif malurez,
Car je suy a Jhesu Crist epuse e espiritez.

E en dementers que la virgne ces paroles diseit,
Este vus un clarte qui del ciel descendeit.
205  Margarete en la chartre tote resplendisseit,
E la croiz Jhesu Crist dedenz apparisseit,
Un blanl colum sur li se seit.

E luy dist: Margarete tu es bonuree,
Seint angele atendent ta alme, del glore ert corunee,
210  De parais la porte ne te ert mie neie,
Car ta virginite a Deu as ben garde.
Ele rend a Deu graces cum femme senee,
Puis s'est au diable del la chartre tornee.

2*

Ele luy comandad sa nature conter:
215 Il luy prie un poi son pe lever,
Ke il puisse ove luy deliverement parler.
Tote ses males ouvres luy permet a conter.

A virgne son talon un poy sus levad,
Ke il fut e comment out nun tretuit li contad,
220 E en apres Bœlzebub Bebzino sey numad:
De males overes fere dist ke onkes ne cessad.

Ore sez com ay nun, ore orez mun mester:
Jo suy co ke les seinz homes met fors de lur mester;
Quant il deivent veiller jo les fat en mal veiller;
225 Vers ceus qui te resemblent ne puis espleter,
Curceus e dolent m'estoit repeirer.

Vencu m'as Margarete, vers tey ne pois durer:
Mes armes sunt freines, vers tey ni les puse porter,
Car jo vey en tey Jhesu Crist parfitement regner.
230 Pur co quant ke tu wous fere te lest Deus esperser.

Tis pere e ta mere mis en peyne ensement,
Ensemble ove mei viverunt en enfern le pulend.
De tei ke lur filie es curuce si fortment
Que par tey sui vencu qui en Deus creis vereiment.

235 Margarete respund: de mei quei te enchandrat,
E ke les seintes ovres agraventer te lessat.
E luy estuveit dire co ke ele luy commandat,
Sa vie e sa virtu tretuit luy demandat,
Dunc est arme de fey, e Deus garde luy ad.
240 Ki ele est e ses ovres puis luy demandad.

Margarete respund que en Deu s'afie:
Ne est dreit que digne chose te resent ne die,
Grace Deu ke sui tel ne te celerai mie.
Cil reddist encontre de sa grant felonie:

245 Satanas est nostre mestre, Dampnedeu le maudie,
De parais chai par sa grant felonie;
Ou ke il wout nus enveit, partuit veit epie,
Quant il trove nus hom qui seit de seincte vie
Luy agueite e manasce e de mort le defie.

250 Angles de seintors nus sout l'um apeller;
Quant orad nostre mestre de ta bonte parler,
E que Ruffin as mort, ne porra mes durer.
Sachez que en awant ne puis a tey parler,
Car jo sent bien en tey Seint Esperist converser.

255 Ancele Dampnedeu jo te pri e requer,
Un poi de ma cervele tun pe moi alascher:
De tut ne me destruie que travail en ai fer:
En tel liu m'en envei u nen ai mester,
Ou ne pousse mes ne nuire ne aider.

260 La bele Margarete poit consentir.
La terre comandeit abair e tost overir:
Le diable fait enz par grant veie saillir.
Cist ne porra jammes a crestien nuisir.
Teu sengor dewum nus tuz aurer e servir,
265 Ke si seit ses fideus garder e mentennir.

Ore est venu lui terme k'ele sera pene.
Li fel Olibrius l'ad tot demande:
Quant issi de la chartre a Deu s'est commande:
A grant turbes la suvit la gent de la contree
270 Que voudrunt esgarder cum ele serad penee.

Veant le provost vint, ne pout plus demorer.
Que se veirs deu aurt prie lui a consentir.
Cele lurt respunt que le pople l'oeit cler:
Chestif mult meuz te wausist celui aurer
275 Qui tut a fet ce mund e cel e terre e mer
Que te deus qui ne oent ne ne pount parler.
Quant li provost l'entend n'i out ke corrucer.

Dunc la fist despuillier e sus en l'eire lever,
Deable pars lur commanda lampes alumer,
280   Que tuit le cors lui puissent arder e embruler.

Cil ne se targerent a ki il fu commandee,
E deame pars le costez ont le fu aioste:
A hunte la demeneit par lur grant cruelte.
Cele en dementers sa oreisun ad fet ad De:
285   Sire bruilliez mon cors par ta grant pite,
Que en mei ne seit truve nul iniquite.

Le provost lui ad dist: Margarete creras,
E a mes deus puans sacrifieras.
Dunc respund Margarete: a ce ne me meurras;
290   Quar ta deitez mult haz que tu tant cher as.

Un grant vaissel de ewe donc il fet aporter,
Liez e pez e meyns la fist einz trebucher,
Par sa grant irreisun iloc la wout neer:
Mes ele commenceit Deu forment a prier;
295   En lui ad se essperance e tut sun recoverer.

E Deus ke tuz jurs regnes en parmanabletez,
Del pople qui ci est qui tun nun seit glorifiez:
Sire moy par ta grant poestez,
Sacez qui par pour ne le t'ai pas ruvez,
300   Mes pur co que ce pople veingne a crestienez.
E facent sacrifise par bone voluntez.

Un bland colum sor sa epaule li sist,
E ce fu lui Seint Espirist ke lui trammit,
Pur lui conforter que rien ne cremist,
305   E pur lui delier que seine s'en issit.

Quant deliez fu graces a Deu en rend,
Del wessel s'en issi veanz tuz erraument.
Sire Deu dune me as virtu e ensement,
Mult m'as ben garde, si t'en gracie fortment:

310    De mey as fet honor e glorifitement:
       Beneit seies tu qui es sanz finement.

       Une voiz luy ad dite: beneite seras,
       Car ta virginite a Deu ben garde as;
       Vien el regne du ciel, iloc reposeras,
315    De vie parmenable corrune seras.
       Cinc milier de la gent creit ingnele pas,
       Estre assez des autres que numer ne puis pas.

       Olibrius co veit, fortment s'en corrucat:
       Tretuiz de meintenant decoler fet les ad.
320    Apres ingnelement ses sergans apellad:
       Penez moy Margarete, jammes ne garrad,
       De la teste trencher mes respit ne averad.
       Cil le firent tost quant il le commandat.

       Fors de la cite la unt inelepas mene;
325    Malcus out nun li serf a ki ele fu liveree;
       Le col li ruve estendre si ad traite l'espee,
       Sanz autre demorance ja la ust decole,
       Quant de la croiz celestre la vist avirune.

       Grant pour oust li serf, merci prist a crier,
330    Cele luy respundi quant issi l'oet parler:
       Tu neis e si m'essaies entor mei converser,
       E tu me cries merci e me wous decoler;
       Ne de omicide fere ne wous onkes cesser;
       Mes tu me dune espace que je me puisse ourer,
335    E cil le octrad car ne le osat deneer.

       Quant Malcus de ourer la oust fet ottreiment
       Vers le ciel regarde, Deu preiad ducement:
       Deu qui feis le ciel e la terre ensement,
       Sire oez ma priere par tun commandement;
340    Ki la vie de moy lirra bonement,
       E de ma passiun fra remembrement,

Ki a my eglise dorad enluminemet,
De tretuz lur pecchez fai alegement.

Unkore te requier jo, cum le men seingor,
345   Ky my iglise frat e averterad en amor,
Ke ma passiun escriverat e averad en honur,
Sire rempliez lur de spirital amur,
De povrete l'engentez e par tut le sucur.

E si acune femme ne pout emfanter,
350   E face mun martire dewant luy reconter,
E par bone creance me woudrat reclammer,
Bel Sire succur la, ne la lessez pener,
Ke si enfes ne seit muz ne awoglez.
Nule rien mes ki dreit n'i puse l'um truver.

355   Dementers ke la virgne cest oreisun dist,
Mult fort prist a toneir e grant horage fit.
Dunc n'i oust si hardi qui de parler se tenist,
Ne meimes Margarete, qui terre ne chaist.
Estevus un colum qui belement la prist,
360   Ducement le levat, e apres li dist:

Tu es bonuree: oyanz tuz dist lui ad:
Nent en en parays deweez ne te serad;
Quant qui as demande Deu ottreie le ad;
Ki meindrat en tristur par tei leesce averad;
365   La ou ta passiun e ton livere serad,
Fudre ne tempeste ne mal n'i avendrat,
Ne malignes espiriz converser ne porrad.

Ele flechist ses genuz, Deus en ad merciez,
Puis al macecren de fe ferir enortez.
370   Nun frai, fet il, Deu ad ove tey parlez.
Ele dist: si tu ne fais ja n'averas part en Deus.
A ceste paroles sa espee a sus levez,
Le chief del bu lui ad meintenant trenchez.
Ore en prent Deu l'arme qui le cors est fineez.

375 Od le alme li angele vers le ciel wont chantant:
Nus hom set la joie k'il wont demenant.
Contre co lui diable wont irrez e plurant.
Teophilus cuilli de lui le remanant,
En un escrin de marbre le respunt meintenant;
380 Par celui sumes nus de la geste sawant,
Il escrist le livere sy se mist avant.

Cil ke la oust decole a pez lui est chait;
Pur co que il ad fet que paresche ne lui seit,
Seint angele pristrunt la alme, el ciel la porterunt dreit.
385 La meinnee de infern de autre part seeit,
Honeint forment e criernt, que le pople le oeit;
Dient que lui lui Deus est grant en ki la virgne creeit.

Tut cil qui sunt priss de divers enfermetez,
Mult sunt awogles, desirus de sauntez,
390 De lui quant parler oient ilec sunt alez:
Dec'il tochent le cors sempres sunt mundez;
Ne sentent puis nul mal ne nul enfermentez.

Es kalendes de Aüst del siecle trepassat,
Quant l'um en cest siecle de lui memorie frat.
395 Deu cum gloriusement sum martire finat.
Dreiz est que od Deu seit, car ben de servir l'ad,
Si est ele sanz dotance, jammes ne partirat.

Ele deprie Deu qui est sanz mentir,
Ke il nus gard de tuz maus, e nus doint deservir,
400 Quant les ames de nus deivent del cors partir,
Quant a sa companie puissuns parvenir,
Qui vivit et regnat Deus per omnia secula seculorum.
Amen.

# Notes.

(M = suggestion of P. Meyer; J = Joly; B.M. = British Museum; B.N. = Bibl. Nationale [Paris].)

---

2.  read **E veant** (M).

8.  read **troveint** (M). The fact that **seyt** is in the present needs no comment, the principle of sequence of tenses, as now understood, not being strictly observed in the old language. Cf. Clédat, Grammaire Elémentaire de la Vieille Langue Française. §§ 468, 9.

13. for **des** read **de**.

14. supply **dunt** after the caesura (M).

21. **Deus** is found in assonance with **-é** (Lat. a) in Alexis and all chansons de geste. (Cf. Alexis 51.)

22. **Theodorus**. The Latin Mss. have Theodosius, which is preserved generally throughout the various versions.
    **Cremout**. This form, according to Burguy, is not found before 1260.

23. Metrical Considerations suggest transposition of the words **en Deu**. En is then **inde**.

24. read **ha-eit**. **Envers** is here used in the sense "compared with". For further examples of this use see Clédat § 550 and Godefroy.

25. **ert nez** is evidently an addition made by some copyist, and its retention is opposed both by sense and metre.

27. read **ha-eit** as in 24. **pounee** should be **posnee**. Burguy gives a form **ponee**. Perhaps we should read **ponnee**.
    **De co secle**. This adjectival use of **co** is frequent in later anglo-norman, and it is even used with nouns in the plural. For Examples cf. Suchier, Reimpredigt p. 107. and cf. 'chou cose' in Fornival's 'Poissance d'Amours' (as quoted by Godefroy).

28. **En luy**. The sense would seem to require **en Deu**.

30. **Dec'** i. e. **de ce** (**de co**).

33. "A propos **d'Olibrius** il est à remarquer que c'est probablement du persécuteur de Sainte Marguerite, autant que du dernier et faible héritier de la pourpre romaine, qu'est venue la renommée proverbiale attachée à ce nom" (J).
    **e** after the caesura must be omitted.
    **emvie**. Not only before **p** and **b**, but also before **f** and **v**, **n** is frequently represented by **m**. Cf. **emfern** 43, 101 &c. So **emfes**, **emfant** &c. (see Alexis p. 102).

34. **finat**. It is especially characteristic of Anglonorman Texts that a large number of verbs alternate between the conjugation in **-ir** and the weak conjugation in **-er**. This occurs especially in the infinitive, past participle,

and third person plural of the preterite. In Alexis we have **avoglir** and **avogler**. In 'Deu le omnipotent' **consentir** and **escopir** suffer like modifications. In 272 of our text it is evident that the author wrote **consenter**, and the scribe writes **siflyr** in 173. In the 'Destruction de Rome' we have **granté** for **garanti**.

38. **unce.** The Latin Mss. have **quindecim**, which is preserved generally in the romance and other derived versions.

39. **ki** i. e. **cui** (a ki).

40. for **le** read **la.**

42. **finist** see note on 34.

46. This may be a corruption of **Ele l'amout assez plus ke cele ki en gist** which follows the idea of v. 40. The Ms. has iglist.

47. Omit **e** after caesura, and read **la** for **le** as in v. 40.

48 & 112. **bien être de** "to be in favour with" (cf. Chron. des Ducs de Norm. II. 1476).

49. The orthography **des i** instead of the usual **de si** is sufficiently defended by Suchier (Reimpredigt p. 75). He points out that the derivation is **de ipso** (not **de ex**) and **ibi** (or **hic**).

58. **Les vellies** should be **les owaillyes** (adopting the orthography of line 89).

59. **Chimin.** The **-e** has become **-i** before the accented **-i** following. Cf. Suchier, Deu le omnipotent 32, **Di pire matire**, and page 107.

   **tirant** should be **tiranz** (tirans); satisfying both rhyme and grammar.

62.
66. } for **ele** read **est.**

69. **aseinement** i. e. **as(s)enement.** Cf. L. du L. quoted by Godefroy "Je iray tant . . . qui Dieu m'en donnera aulcun assignement". Ducange gives a form **assinamentum** (for **aisiamentum**).

72. Identity of rhyme-words is not an uncommon phenomenon in Old French. In our text we have also **tencun** (94, 95). In this line (72) I am inclined to suspect a copyist's error, and would read **sanz finement** for **parfitement** (cf. l. 311).

74. This line is corrupt. Perhaps the last copyist found "**mult irez s'en alerent**".

76. read **l'ont.**

77. Godefroy quotes **erreement** from the Grenoble Ms. of Artur.

78. read **o luy** or **a luy** (omitting **il**). This assumes the scribe to have intended **gire** (gésir). But the original is more likely to have read **luy estoveit gehir**, which satisfies the rhyme.

79. read **la,** and the metre requires **ferad.**

81. read **la butent e decirent.** In St. Auban (Atkinson) we find **desirer,** in Josaphaz **decirer.**

87. **tes intime nuns** a copyist's error for **tun sentime nuns.** Concerning the rhymes of this strophe see introduction.

97. **creatur** (see introduction). A careless scribe might easily have written it for **traïtur** (trisyllable: Cf. G. de Montreuil, Roman de la Violette 1475).

100. for **lur** read **luy.**

101. read **sofre.** This and the preceding correction are suggested by v. 98.

102. read **li** for **luy.**

106. This neuter use of **cel** is not infrequent in Agn. Cf. P. de Thaün's Computus v. 111 (Ed. Mall); Reimpredigt (Suchier) 35. f. &c. Cf. also **cest** (Computus 55).

107. read **k'il ne les puisse.**

116. The metre requires **diez** (as **facez** 120) to be in the Singular.

124. **de** for **dei** (debeo). Our author wrote **aver** for **aveir** (144).

129. The peculiar spelling oreillie (cf. **owaillye** 58, 89, **narillie** 170) seems to represent the 'mouillé' sound of the **l.**

132. **Le richies** read **Le riches** (i. e. Deu).

133. read **a mes plaies.** The metre then requires **mecine,** of which **medicine** is a later equivalent first introduced in the XIII th Cy, and taken direct from the Latin.

135. **metnee.** Norman **mednee** for mesnee. We find **adne** for asne in the "Livres des Rois".

     **finir** in this sense only used negatively.

136. for **pelstrine** read **peitrine.** The **s** is an intercalation of a scribe.

138. read **commence** for the sake of the metre, and of consistency with **veit.**

143. **mostrer** leaves much to be desired in the matter of sense. Although the word **monestement** exists, I have not found a corresponding verb **monester** which seems to have been intended by an earlier scribe. **Amonester** might be supplied, but the line then exceeds even anglonorman license.
     Suchier's quotation from the Life of St. Modwenna (Ueber Atkinson's Vie de St. Auban) would give parallels for an orthography
     . . . **ducement a 'monester.**

145. read **irez.**

151. **spirital** cf. (St. Auban) **li angres espiriteus.**

152. read **macecrier:** cf. Vie de S^te. Marguerite (Ms. de Chartres) "au macacrier dist lieement". The form **macecren** (which occurs twice in our text) is not found elsewhere, and is a copyist's error. Godefroy gives many variant forms of the word.

153. for **li** read **le.**

169. see note 129 for **narillies.** For this form of the word cf. Gloss de Salins (quoted by Godefroy). "**nariller:** frouter les narilles."

173. for **siflyr** read sifler.

176. This line is corrupt. I suggest
     **Que avisonkes pout desor ses pez ester.**

180. omit **-e** after caesura.

182. read **se garnist.**

183. read **li draguns** and **se fendist.**

184. **halegree** cf. Horn 4935 (Michel) quoted by Godefroy, and Légende de Théophile (Bartsch) 759.

186. read **al es. A son fenestre.** This reading is probably occasioned by a too casual perusal of the Latin Ms. Mm. IV, 6 (Camb) has "aspiciebat

in **sinistram** partem carceris, et ecce vidit" &c. A few lines earlier we have "nutrix aspiciebat per **fenestram**, et orationes eius scribebat".

187. for **leid** read **leidde**, which also restores the metre.

188. Consultation of Latin and other versions suggests the change of **cheffuz** into **genuz.**
The Latin has "manus suas ad genua colligatas". The O. E. Text of the late XII th Cy (Cockayne: Narratiunculae) has "his honda to his cneowum gebundenne". The Scotch Version has "with handis bundine til his kneis".

198. read **te destruie J. C.** A copyist had added **tut** (cf. 200).

199. for **m'est** read **s'est.** For rhymes of this strophe see introduction.

207. read **blans.**

217. The sense seems to recommend **promet.**

218. Read **La virgne,** which begins a new strophe.

220. It is interesting to compare the various versions here: The Latin Ms. B. N. 17002 (X th Cy) quoted by Joly reads '**Behel** est nomen mihi'. Ms. Camb. Mm. IV, 6 (XIII th Cy) 'post **Belzebub** princeps fui'. Wace's text (Joly) '**Belsabut** ai a non'. The Ms. B. N. 19525 has **Belzebu.** The O. E. Ms., formerly in Trin. Coll. Library (Camb), published by Hickes (I 224) and by Horstmann — the original of which is of the XIII th Cy — reads **Belsebug.** The Ms. Bodl 34 (B) 'ich habbe efter **Beelzebub** mest monnes bone ibeon'. The Paris Ms. B. N. 11705 (quoted by Joly) has '**Bezel** est nomen mihi; post **Behelzebu** ego'. Two English versions (Auchinl. & Ashm. 61, Ed. Horstmann) have **Belgys.** The Prague Ms. reads 'ich heize **Beliäl,** ouch **Belezepuop** est mîn mâl'.
Our text would seem based on the Version found in Ms. Paris 11705, and to have a common source with Ms. Bodl. 34. But it has been sufficiently demonstrated that the Camb Ms. Mm. IV. 6. may be regarded as practically identical with the version from which this text is derived.

222. **ore.** The Ms. has a contracted form which, if expanded, would give **orrea. ore** is evidently intended.

224. read **fac.**

228. **freines:** read **freites** (as in Gaimar 439, 935).

230. read **esperer.**

235. read **di.**

236. Ménage writes that, in his time, **acraventer** was still pronounced **agra-venter** in Normandy. Cf. 'Set Dormans' (Koch) 876, Vie de St. Auban (Atkinson) 1700: and Suchier Reimpredigt, p. 71.

239. **armee** (thus corrected) should be placed after **de fey** (for metre's sake).

242. The Latin Text (Camb Mm. IV. 6.) has 'Michi non licet hec nunciare tibi, quia non dignus es audire vocem meam'. If for **resent** we read **resconse** or **reconte** the sense still leaves much to be desired. Perhaps we should read **cele chose.**

244. For **encontre** read **encore.**

247. The sense and metre require **e** before **epie.**

250. This line, as it stands, is unintelligible. **De seintors** seems to be an error for **deserites** or **desenores.**

252. **Ruffin**: Lat. Ms. **Rufonem**. Other versions **Rufum, Ruffon, Ruffines, Ruphins**. Ms. Ashm. 61 has **Geffron**.

252. **mourir** is also used transitively in 289.

261. read **a baer**.

266. read **le** for **lui**.

267. read **tost**.

269. The Ms. has **seuvit**. Read **sivit**. But the Brit. Mus. Cott. Ms. of Josaphaz has **seuvissent** which Koch reads **sewissent**.

272. **consentir** should be **consenter**, see note on 34.

273. read **luy**.

279. read **D'ambes pars** and insert **a** after **lampes**.

281. omit **il**.

282. read **E d'ambes pars** as in 279.

295. read **s'esperance**.

298. The sense requires **meintenez moy** (cf. v. 86).

300. read **crestientez** (i. e. crestiente: cf. voluntez 301).

301. cf. note on 59.

302. **bland** for **blans**. Perhaps by unconscious analogy to **blond** (cf. **blund** St. Auban 640).

303. omit **lul** and insert **le** before the second **lui**.
read **trammist**. The Ms. has **trammiljt**.

316. **Cinc milier**. Most of the versions agree in this computation, and, where any vary, it has been in order to accomodate the number to a requisite rhyme or metre. E. g. (Hickes).

> "Ther bileveden on J C **a thousand ant five**
> Al withouten children, ant withouten wive."

**ingnele** (and **veingne** 300). The first **n** is a sign of the 'mouillé' sound.

319. Other versions localise the massacre more or less accurately. Ms. Harl 2801 has "in Decapoli et Armeniã civitate". Mm. IV. 6. has "in campo lim et Armenia". Ms. Bodl 34 has "in an burh of Armenie Caplinfet inempnet", an evident corruption of the above mentioned reading. The B. N. Ms. 1555 has "ou champ c'on apele Lymet". pointing to the same error. The O. E. text printed by Cockayne in his 'Narratiunculae' reads "in Limes feold". An interesting fiction, based on a false reading of this passage in a Seville Breviary, is referred to in the sketch of the history of the Legend.

321. **Penez**. A strict expansion of the Ms. brachygraph would give **preenez**. It seems to be a similar error to that in v. 222.
**garrad** should be **garirad** which rectifies the metre also.

325. **Malcus**. This name is common to nearly all the versions. A few give no name at all.

331. read **tu me neis e essaies** (neis = nei-es. The diphthong is found simplified in Reimpredigt 23 [text C]).

334. omit **me**.

345,6. The sense would be improved, and the metre rectified by reading:

> "Ky my iglise frat e averad en honur,
> E ke ma passiun escrivrat en amor . ." etc.

347. for **lur** read **le.**
348. read **De povrete l'en getez.** This redundant **en** is not uncommon. Cf. St. Auban 119 &c. where Atkinson prints **engetter.** But is should be printed as two words. Cf. Suchier, Reimpredigt 5, 7.
356. read **fist.**
357. This line is not devoid of sense, but I am inclined to think that the author probably wrote something else. I would suggest
'**qui parler ne cremist'.**
358. insert **a** before **terre** and omit **ne.**
362. omit one **en.**
369. read **a le** and omit **le.**
374. **arme.** This form in Wace "Quant il ot ce dit, jus cheï Leis la virgne, **l'arme rendi**" gave rise to a curious misunderstanding in later versions. E. g. B. N. 1555 "jouste lui chiet tantost l'espee"! (J.)
377. read **li diable.**
368. **Teophilus.** The Latin Mss. have **Theotimus** (Theotinus). Wace has **Theodimus,** the Scotch Version **Theophine.** Ms. Auchinl **Theodosius.** Bodl Ms. **Theochimus.** B. N. 1555 follows the Latin.
381. read **e si le mist avant** cf. Deu le omnipotent 24. c.
382. read **cha-eit.**
383. If we are to retain **paresche** (pigritia) the meaning would be "that his reward might not be delayed". Perhaps **pesche** should be read; "that sin should not be imputed to him".
385. Can **ponnee podnee** be analogous to **melnnee mednee?**
386. read **crieint.**
387. for **lui lui** read **li.**
388. for **priss** read **pris.**
396. read **deservi** (M.)
401. for **Quant** read **que** (M.)

## Suggestions for restitution of the Original Metre.

2. **e** initial (M). 3. **e sentes.** 9. **esteit il** (M). 12. **ore en est** (M). 14. **dunt me** (M). 15. **le son** (M). 18. **trayez vus** (M). 23. **Creeint deu en out.** 24. **haeit.** 25. (ert nez). 26. **e sage.** 27. **haeit.** 33. **l'occist par.** 40. **cum si la oust portee.** 42. **or quant.** 43. **ele alad.** 44. **trove.** 46. see note. 47. (e). 51. (ele). 52. **passiuns oeit de martirs.** 53. (e). 54. initial **e.** 56. **partirat.** 57. **icel.** 58. **ovellies.** 59. **mult mauveys.** 60. **a ses culverz.** 64. or initial. 67. (ele). 74. (il): **oieient: mult irez s'en aierent.** 75. **d'iloc.** 78. (il). 79. **ferad.** 80. **nule demorance.** 81. **La butent...icil.** 83. **ke ele...anguisse en ad.** 84. or initial. 90. **mes** initial. 96. **ay nun.** 98. **ke en ...un li men auncessur.** 101. or **sofre.** 102. (si). 103. **serer** or **commande.** 107. **k'il ne les pusse:** (grevement) or write **graventer** and omit tormenter. 116. **dies** and **perdray.** 117. (e) after caesura. 120. **faces.** 123. **deinad li**

sire a mort son cors livrer. 127. commenca. 133. or envey a mes plaies
mecine. 134. (en). 138. commence. 140. Crei mes deus Marg. e (cf. Ms.
B. N. 19525). 142. il veient. 151. ele est. 152. acertes. 155. e initial.
158. feray. 159. si cum. 161. ma alme. 166. (o). 168. e russe.
169. e sez ouz. 172. e initial or unë and destre main. 175. quant si.
176. Que avisonkes pout desor. 179. ke ne li. 180. (e) and (en) initial.
181. le livre. 184. (seinne). 185. (ele). 187. leidde. 191. e deus.
192. le sun. 198. te destruie. 201. (tu): maleürez. 202. car suy ... spiritez.
203. (e en). 207. es vus un b. c. ki sur li se se - eit. 208. boneüree.
212. si cum. 213. puis apres. 215. de luy lever. 218. La virgne ... un
poy de luy levad. 219. ke fut e com out nun trestuil il li contad. 220. (en).
221. onc. 223. (les). 224. (en). 225. ne puis ren. 226. mes initial and
m'en estolt. 228. initial or and nes pois. 229. (Car jo). 230. (tu). 234.
qu'en or (en). 236. graventer. 239. de fey armee. 240. puis il. 241. se.
242. resconse. 244. e ciL 247. e epie. 250. deserites. 254. for esperist
as dissyllable cf. St. Brandan 131. 258. nul mester. 259. pousse je. 260.
or luy polt. 261. baer. 262. initial e. 264. (nus). 267. la ad. 269. a
turbes. 273. mes cele lui. 274. (mult): icel deu aurer. 279. d'ambes pars
commanda lampes a alumer. 281. e cil: (il). 282. D'ambes pars. 284. s'oreisun fet. 285. mult grant. 286. nule. 288. or after caesura. 290. cheres.
295. s'esperance. 297. Del pople qui ci est seies glorifiez. 298. meintenez
moy (from 86). 302. Es vus initial. 303. ce fu S. E. ke deu a luy trammist.
304. reconforter: de rien. 306. quant ele. 309. me as. 315. corrunee.
316. cre - eint. 321. garirad. 323. e cil. 330. quant si. 331. tu me neis
e essaies. 334. (tu) (me). 335. octread: (car). 337. regardat. 340. mult
bonement. 341. fera. 342. e ki. 343. fai lor. 344. for jo read si. 345.
346. Ky my Iglise frat e averad en honur, E ki ma passiun escriverat en amor.
348. De povrete le getez. 349. porra. 353. ne muz. 355. ceste. 357. qui
parler ne cremist. 358. qui a terre chaïst, 360. en apres. 361. boneüree.
362. ne nent en parays: (ne). 368. a le: (fe). 370. nun le ferai. 373.
demeintenant. 374. la arme. 376. ne set ... ke il. 381. e si le. 382. chaeit.
383. pesche. 384. pristrent: porterent. 386. e honeint e crieint. 387. cil
deus and creit or (en). 388. icil and enfertez (cf. Blondel de Neele 'Quant
je plus sui' v. 74). 389. dunt mult. 390. s'en sunt alez. 391. tuz mundez.
392. nules enfertez. 398. qui tut est. 401. nus puissuns.

# History of the Legend.

It is not difficult to fix, at least approximately, the time of the occurrences recorded in the Legend of St. Margaret. The great Antiochian persecution during which the presbyter Lucius suffered martyrdom took place under the joint rule of Diocletian and Maximian.

Maximin was entrusted in 305 with the sovereignty of Syria and Egypt, and, on the death of Galerius, he added to his provinces that of Asia Minor. Between the date 305 and that of Maximin's death (313) the martyrdom of St. Margaret, if we are to grant its historic existence, must certainly fall. That we have no historic record of it is not surprising; the occurrence in its unvarnished actuality was commonplace in such an epoch of wholesale martyrdom; and, further, it was the policy of the persecutors to destroy all the writings of their Christian victims, so that the events in question were probably recorded according to hearsay evidence at some later period. The supernatural accessories of the story are found in the earliest forms in which it has been preserved to us. In establishing the date the manuscripts do not give much assistance beyond that afforded by the incidents recorded. The earliest manuscripts had probably no date assigned, for any such information is wanting in nearly all the manuscripts which are at our disposal. An exception is the Latin manuscript B. M. Ar 169 (XIII[th] Cy.) which begins "Annorum ab incarnatione domini salvatoris fere ducentorum nonaginta circulus volvebatur". It seems probable that this is an original addition by some scribe who had made for himself the

3

necessary historic researches. The English version MS. Harl
2277 (XIV th Cy.) reads:
"Lither was themperor Diocletian,
"Lither was his felawe ek, that het Maximian."
An old English alliterative version (MS. Bodl. 34) gives
the date of the month, following, no doubt, the day and
month for which the life appointed in the Latin Passionals
ʋ was that of St. Margaret. The MS. reads "i the moneth that
on ure ledene is ald englisch efterlith, inempnet iulius o latin,
o the twentuthe dei" (Cockayne E. E. T. S. no. 13). The MS.
Ashm. (printed by Horstmann, Altenglische Legenden) adds a
detail which is almost humorous:
"On a tewysdey sche was quyke and dede."
Further notice as to date I have not discovered in any of the
many versions consulted. It remains then to ascertain the date
approximately by independent historic evidence, which gives
as superior and inferior limits the years 305 and 313.

The story is an oriental one and, in any effort to trace
its development, it is to the East that we must look for its
original form, and for any collateral evidence as to its authenticity. Such evidence is however not forthcoming. The oldest
Syrian Martyrology extant (MS. addit. 12150 published by
Wright in the Journal of Sacred Literature VIII, 45) although
assigning many martyrs and confessors to the town of Antioch,
includes no reference to our saint. Had such a reference
been there, it would have assisted very materially to establish
the authenticity of the legend, but, on the other hand, the
mutilated state of the manuscript absolves us from the conclusion that Saint Margaret was not acknowledged at the
epoch of its composition. We have, however, evidence that to the
Greek church this legend was not unknown. Symeon Metaphrastes (X th Cy.) as quoted by Surius (Venice 1581, IV, 86)
reads: "Marina, quam latinae ecclesiae Margaritam vocant",
and this double nomenclature accompanies the legend in many
of its developments. In the British Museum Library there is
a Greek version of the life of St. Marina, dating however

only from the XVI[th] Century (25881). But it is to the Latin church, and to the revival of letters under Charlemagne that we must refer the first extensive development of the legend as it is preserved to us. The life of St. Margaret of Antioch was assigned to the date XIV Kal. Aug. in the Latin Passionals, and the life of St. Marina — identical in all points with the former — is often given a few pages earlier at the date III Id. Jul., the order being sometimes reversed.

Rabanus (IX[th] Cy.) gives a brief life of the saint, mentioning all the salient points of the expanded legend; "vinculae, carceres, flagella, equuleum, diabolus in draconis specie, similiter et in aethiopis" &c. In the Martyrology of Usuardus (IX[th] Cy.) at the date XIII Kal. Aug. Migne records a marginal reading (probably a later interpolation): "Eodem die sanctae ... garitae virginis et martiris." It must have been during this and the following century that St. Margaret gradually obtained a permanent place in the western martyrologies, for although Ado (IX[th] Cy.) and Aelfric (X[th] Cy.) do not mention her name, Notker (circ. 1000) includes her among the martyrs, and assigns her the date III Id. Jul. (Migne CXXXI, 1119), and the testimony of Rabanus has already been adduced. It is certain that from this period the Passio. St. Margaretae was found in the library of most monasteries, and its diffusion followed close on that of the Christian religion itself. Latin texts of the legend abound in many countries — in the British Museum alone there are 16, exclusive of those contained in collections — and amply attest the popularity of the story: we shall presently see how these versions have been everywhere followed by versions in the vernacular. The legend was also reproduced in many Latin Hymns of the middle ages, and of the Renaissance, especially in Italy.

It must here be remarked that, though the sensational and supernatural details were to be found in the earliest forms of the legend, they were, by many, sceptically regarded from the first. Symeon Metaphrastes discounted them as the malicious invention of scoffers, if not of the evil one himself: "a genti-

libus forte, aut ab haereticis et profanis, et veritatis intelligentia privatis viris . . . pravae ac sceleratae mentis execranda figmenta, ad Christi et sanctorum eius contumeliam composita". Jacobus a Voragine (circa 1250) in the Golden Legend (Graesse, Leipzig 1850) has also: "istud autem quod dicitur de draconis devoratione, et ipsius crepatione, apocryphum et frivolum reputatur". The Bollandists have also adhered to this judgment in their Acta SS.

To attempt a descriptive catalogue of the old French MSS. in which some form of this legend is found would be beyond the limits of this essay. So far back as 1875 P. Meyer indicates the existence of at least four rhymed versions, one of which occurs in thirty manuscripts.

In the library of Tours there exists a copy of a version by Wace, which has been fully described by Luzarche (1873) and edited by Joly (1879). It contains about 420 lines of 8-syllable verse, the first part of the poem being wanting. This manuscript appeared to Joly to contain a unique copy of the version: he assigns the date 1250 to the copy, and places the original 50 years earlier. But P. Meyer (Romania VIII, 275) indicates the existence of a complete copy of Wace's Version of which he quotes the opening lines. As an appendix to Joly's Edition (Vieweg, Paris 1879) we find the text of the MS. B. N. 19525, written at the end of the XIII<sup>th</sup> Century, also in octosyllabic verse, and which the editor claims to have Wace for its source. He adds further the text of the MS. B. N. 1555 (early XV<sup>th</sup> Cy.), an octosyllabic version with signs of a different origin. Both these latter were edited by Scheler (Antwerp 1877). In the "Bulletin du Bibliophile Belge" (Vol. IV, 1847) we find an old French rhymed version, communicated by Baron Léon de Herkenrode, and copied by him from a manuscript which had evidently been used as an amulet. Sixteen years later (Hannover 1863) a slightly varying copy of the same version was published by W. L. Holland. This editor does not seem to have been aware of the earlier publication of his version, as an appendix to which he prints

a German prose version of the XV<sup>th</sup> Century. He also draws
attention to a middle-dutch version published in the Belgisch
Museum (Ghent 1837), the existence of which corroborates
Joly's statement as to the popularity of the legend in Belgium.

Joly indicates 10 manuscript copies (Bibl. Nat.) of various
forms of the legend, three of which date from the XIII<sup>th</sup> and
the rest from the XIV<sup>th</sup> and XV<sup>th</sup> Centuries. He also mentions
two XV<sup>h</sup> Century MSS. in the Bibl. de l'Arsenal, and three
prose versions (XIII, XIV, XV<sup>th</sup> Cent.) in the Bibl. Nationale.

There are in the British Museum Library various versions
of the legend, both in prose and in verse, none of which
however afford very special assistance for the critical consi-
deration of the Cambridge MS. These are Dom. d. XI, 8,
Harl. 2947, Sloane 1611, all in verse: and Reg. 20, D. VI. 46,
a life of St. Marina in prose.

The library of York Minster contains an Anglonorman
version of the legend in Alexandrine verses arranged in
'laisses monorimes', as in the Cambridge version Ee. VI. XI.
But the two poems differ widely in their general style, and
in their treatment of the common material. One leaf of the
York Ms. is partially mutilated, the complete poem containing
about 440 lines, and dating, in its present form, from the early
XIV<sup>th</sup> Century. My transcription of the text will shortly be
published in "Modern Language Notes", and I therefore abstain
from any detailed description of what is, from many points
of view, a most interesting poem.

The popularity of the legend did not cease with the
invention of printing, for there exist many printed versions
both in prose and in verse. Brunet mentions eight verse
editions, all published about the year 1500.

If any further proof of its popularity were needed, we
have it in the existence of a provençal version. In 1875
(P. Meyer, Rom. IV, 482) there were only seven known lives
of saints in the southern vernacular, and one of these saints
was St. Margaret, a provençal version of whose 'passion' in
octosyllabic verse was published in that year by Noulet

(Toulouse). A propos of this edition, P. Meyer indicates the existence of a parallel and more correct provençal text in Stockholm, by the aid of which he is enabled to correct the text published by Noulet.

In Italy Saint Margaret was among the most widely venerated saints of the middle ages. Tradition indeed asserts that her remains were conveyed to Brindisi, and found a final resting place at Montefiascone. Lambecius (Comment. de Biblioth. Vindobon. 1669, Vol II) indicates "Volumen membranaceum in quarto, multis imaginibus exornatum, quo continetur (1) Vita et Passio S. Margaretae virginis et martyris, composita antiquis rhythmis Italicis". Its opening lines, which he quotes, are:

> Omniomo intende e staga impace,
> Chi vole oldire de uno sermone verace,
> De una legenda molto bella
> De una sanctissima ponzella,
> Che multo fu fidele a Deo
> E lo spirito sancto fu in leo.
> Ela haveve nome Malgarita.

In the British Museum (MS. Harl 5347) we have an Italian verse life of the late XIV<sup>th</sup> Cy. ascribed to a certain Tectino, but only differing from the last mentioned version by the addition of an introduction which has hitherto served to conceal the identity of the two poems from the too superficial observer. It is brilliantly, if not artistically, illustrated, and contains some 1200 lines. To the further development of this legend in Italy I shall refer again later. Graesse mentions printed Italian versions of the XVI<sup>th</sup> Cy.

In Spain too our saint enjoyed great popularity. Florez (España Sagrada, Marin, Madrid 1763) points out that there were 16 churches named after her in the bishopric of Orense alone, besides large numbers in the contiguous sees. L. Pannier (St. Alexis 339) also indicates the existence of Spanish versions of our legend. Florez (Vol XVII) discusses a current ecclesiastical tradition that the scene of the Martyrdom of St. Marina

was a district Limia in Galicia, where, it was alleged, there
had existed towns known as Antiochia and Arminia (later
Armea). Indeed various so-called relics of the saint were
preserved in the neighbourhood of Aguas Santas, the authenticity of which however Florez declares to be doubtful: "del
carballo, de los hornos, y del agujero (incapaz de admitir
cuerpo, ni aun de un niño) ... y otras individualidades que
no tienen mas apoyo que de un vulgo Protéo". The origin
of this fiction was apparently a corrupt reading of the Latin
Text (cf. note on 319). The Seville breviary read: "in campo
Limiae sub urbe Armenia" where the original Latin had "in
Decapoli et urbe Armenia". Florez sums up (XVII, 221) as
follows: "Concluyo en fin que admito una Santa Marina martir
en este obispado (Orense), laqual no tiene conexion con el
presidente Olibrio del oriente, ni con otras particularidades de
la martyrizada en Antioquia de Pisidia: sino que la presente
fue Gallega: pero ignorandose como en otros santos martires
las particularidades de su vida y martirio, la aplicaron las
del Oriente, lo que para ser afirmado de la nuestra, necesita
mas abonadas pruebas."

Nor do we seek in vain among Teutonic nationalities
for the preservation of our legend. We have already remarked
the mention of our saint by Notker of St. Gallen. An old
German version, referred to the XII[th] Cy., was published by
Haupt (from a Berlin MS.) in the Zeitschrift für deutsches
Alterthum I (Leipzig 1841). In Germania (1859, p. 440) Bartsch
has printed another text, the original of which he also refers
to the XII[th] Cy., and which is found in the Prague MS. XVI
G. XIX. A kindred version was discovered by Wagner at
Klosterneuburg, and is discussed and compared with the
Prague version in Germania 1862 (p. 268). While writing
this Essay, I learn that the librarian of the Trier Library
has discovered a fragment of a middle high German verse
legend of St. Margaret for which he claims a higher antiquity
than is assigned to the complete versions above referred to.
Other extant German versions are mentioned by Holland in

his introduction. In the XIV[th] Century Hartwig von dem Hage
made the sufferings of St. Margaret the subject of one of his
poems, as did the English poet Lydgate a century later. In
the first years of the XIV[th] Cy. printed versions were published
in Köln, a reprint of which may be found in Schade's 'Geistliche
Gedichte des XIV. und XV. Jahrhunderts vom Niederrhein'
(Hannover 1854).

Mediaeval English Literature also contributes largely to
the materials at our disposal for establishing the wide-spread
popularity of St. Margaret. An early English prose version,
dating from the XI[th] Century, was published by Cockayne in
his Narratiunculae (1861). For the Early English Text So-
ciety the same writer published (in 1866) various English
versions of the legend. The first (MS. Bodl 34 & others) is
an alliterative poem (date about 1200), and is specially remark-
able as containing an incident invented by its writer, which
has no parallel in any other known version. This portion I
have quoted later in illustration of the variants of the respective
versions. In the same volume Cockayne prints a version in
verse (Harl 2277) executed about 1330 and dating from 1300.
He adds also the version printed by Hicks (Thesaurus I, 224)
from a manuscript formerly in Trin. Coll. Camb. Library, now
in the British Museum, the original of which Horstmann
refers to the early part of the XIII[th] Cy. In Horstmann
(Altenglische Legenden; neue Folge) we have two versions
of the legend (Meidan Margaret) which the editor attributes
to the early XIV[th] and to the middle of the XV[th] Cy. respectively.
The MS. Cantab. Ff. II, 38 contains an English prose version
of the XV[th] Cy., and the legend was also "compendyously
compiled in balade by Lidgate dan John, monk of Bury"
(edited by Horstmann Ae. Leg.).

There remains to be noticed a Scottish version of the
legend, contained in the Cambridge MS. published by Horstmann,
and attributed by the editor (though by no other scholar
of note), to the poet John Barbour. The author, as indeed

in most of the other legends which he treats, draws largely
from the "Aurea Legenda". The introduction, for instance, is
clearly taken from the work of J. a. Voragine. It commences:

> Qwa wil the vertu wyt of stanis
> In the lapidar ma fynd, ane is
> Of thame, that callyt is "Margarit"
> Vertuyse, lytil, clere, and quhyt . . . &c.

But the poet appears to have consulted other versions. Compare (e. g.) "Tyne nocht my sawle with fellone mene" with
Camb. Ee. VI, 11 (v. 88) "ne perdez m'alme ho ces maves
felluns"; and "as a schepe ymang wlfis" with "com owaillye
entre lus". The expanded form of the legend, as compared
with the "Aurea Legenda", shows indeed undoubted signs of
large appropriation from other sources.

Any one who has read the legend of St. Margaret in any
of its more expanded forms cannot wonder at the immense
popularity which it obtained during the middle ages. The
reading of this Passio was said to produce the instant and
safe delivery of women in labour. There is a strange irony
in the process of legend-development by which the resolutely
pure virgin is made to preside graciously over the pains of
child-bed. Joly (p. 26) quotes passages from miracle plays
in illustration of this belief, and Pannier (St. Alexis 339)
draws attention to a passage in Rabelais where Gargamelle
refers superciliously to the reputation of our saint. But the
benefactions of St. Margaret were by no means confined to
gracious presidence over the pangs of parturition. Whoever
wrote a copy of her Passion, or read it in a right spirit, or
even heard it read, was to receive absolution of sin, and of
sin's visible effects in the flesh. Whoever invoked her sincerely
should be heard promptly. And he who dedicated a church,
or even a candle, to her memory should know no limit to the
power of his petition. No saint could possibly enjoy greater
popularity, if popularity depend upon variety of potential
benefaction.

"Vengron horbs, sex e mutz
"Contrayt, glocs, maladobatz,
"Totz partiro d'aqui sanatz" (Noulet: quoted by J.)
And so through all the versions. The credulity of the church
outlived the invention of printing. An Italian copy of the
legend (Venice: XVI<sup>th</sup> Cy.) bears the title "Legenda et oratione
di S. Margherita, historiata; La qual oratione legendola, over
ponendola adosso a una donna che non potesse parturire,
subito parturirà senza pericolo"; and d'Esternod (Espadon
Satyrique) completing the description of a woman who was a
finished hypocrite adds:
        "De sainte Marguerite elle sait la légende."
Even royalty was not behindhand in the cult of our saint.
Joly writes (p. 29), adducing numerous historic examples: "Ce
sont des reines qui successivement proclament la foi des femmes
de France dans l'intervention de la Sainte au moment le plus
critique de leur vie. Elle est à plusieurs reprises solennelle-
ment invoquée pour de royales naissances." He also points
out (p. 23) how much of the painting and sculpture of the
middle ages, and of later times, was inspired by the story of
Margaret's martyrdom, instancing, among other works, a
chef d'œuvre of Raphael, now in the Louvre Gallery. The
pastoral colouring of the legend gave it in the country districts
a popularity equal to that which it obtained among the more
cultured portion of the population. Its sensational incidents
lend themselves easily to rude dramatic form, and about the
year 1500 it was adapted still more to the taste of the masses
by being produced in the form of a Mystery play. For a
description of this particular development in France, it suffices
to refer to the interesting little book of Mr. Joly, who gives
copious extracts from a unique copy in the Bibl. Nationale.
It is highly probable that the same development took place
in other countries. For this conjecture there is due support
in the case of Italy, on the authority of Graesse, who mentions
certain dramatic representations of the Passio, dating from
the XVI<sup>th</sup> Century.

# Some important variants in the Versions.

The various versions of our legend have naturally many minor differences, but there are also certain noteworthy ones which demand a special mention. The Latin manuscripts narrate the tearing of the maiden's flesh with hooks, and this incident is placed after the scourging of her body with rods. With the Latin agree B. N. 19525 (and probably Wace), the MS. Bodl 34, together with the Prague MS., and the Scotch version. In our own text the incident is wanting, as in B. N. 1555 and others.

Further many of the Latin MSS. contain statements of the fiend which are entirely wanting in our version, but which are found in the·Scotch version, Wace, and others. Here however B. N. 19525 agrees with our text, as does B. N. 1555, while Bodl 34 contains part of the speech referred to, but not the whole. I give the Latin from the Camb. MS. Mm. IV, 6. "Sciscitare et vide in libris iamne et mambre (cf. II, Tim. III, 8), ibi autem scrutare, et quod queris percipies. Ibi enim invenies genus nostrum ... Nam et Salomon conclusit nos in uno vase vitreo. Sed in unam partem eiusdem vasis misimus ignem, et venientes babilonii, putaverunt aurum in ipso invenire, et fregerunt vas, et tunc nos, relaxati, replevimus orbem terrarum."

The old English version 'Seinte Marherete' (Bodl 34 &c.) contains a curious original addition by the writer, to wit a wooing scene between "a clean man and a clean woman". I transcribe it in full from Cockayne, whose edition is out of print.

"ich leote other hwiles a cleane mon: wunieu neh a
cleane wummon. that ich toward ham ne warpe ne ne
weorri. ah leote ham talkin ant tauelin of godlec ant
treowliche luvien ham. withuten uvel wilnung ant alle
unwreste willes. that either of otheres as of his ahne beo
trusti. ant treowliche to witene. ant te sikerure beon to
sitten togederes ant gomenin bi ham ane. thenne thurh
this sikerlec seche ich earst uppon ham, ant scheote swithe
dernlich ant wundi er ha witen hit. with swithe attri halewi.
hare unwarie heorte. lihtliche on alre earst. with luveliche lates. with steape bihaldunge either on other. ant
with plohe speche sputte to mare. swa longe that ha
tollith togederes ant toggith. ant thenne thudde ich in
ham luveliche thohtes on earst hare unthonckes ant swa
waxeth that wa thurh that ham hit thuncheth god. ant
thenne ant when ha leteth me. ant he letten me nawt.
ne ne storith hamseolf: ne ne stondeth strongliche agein:
ich leade ham ithe leinen. ant ithe ladliche lake of the
suti sunne. gef ha et stonden wulleth mine unwreste
wrenches ant mine swikele swenges: wrestlin ha moten
ant witherin with ham seolven. ah me akeasten ha ne
mahen. er ha ham seolf overcumen."

In the Latin MS. Mm. IV, 6 and in 'S. Marherete'
the VII[th] hour is indicated as the time when St. Margaret
was cast into the dungeon on the first occasion. This
precision is wanting in the other versions which I have
consulted.

An interesting study is afforded by the varying development of the reading "in domo inclite matrone" the (probably) original Latin localisation of the embalming of
St. Margaret's remains. 'Seinte Marherete' reads "in hire
grandame hus that wes icleopet Clete"! The Camb. MS.
KK. II, 22 reads "sincletice matrone" probably a much earlier
corruption which led to the emendation "simplicie matrone"
(B. N. 17002 and others).

Beyond the variants already discussed there are no important changes in the substance of the Story as found in the various versions. The introduction and conclusion are naturally treated in a very different way in different texts, according to the procedure of the individual writers.

Thus the name of the author of the original Passio appears in various forms — Theotimus, Theotinus, Teophilus, Theodimus, Theophine, Theochimus and even Theodosius — this last reading arising from confusion with the name of St. Margaret's father as found in most of the versions, but which stands in our text as Theodorus.

# The Latin Original.

It has been seen in our sketch of the history of the legend that we have at our disposal a great number of Latin manuscripts containing versions of the life of St. Margaret. Among these the MS. B. N. 17002 dates as far back as the X[th] Cy. In the British Museum there are from fifteen to twenty Latin lives, one of which (Harl 5327) is also of the X[th] Cy., while two others (Ar. 169, and 10050) are not later than the XII[th] Cy. Some of these MSS., it is true, omit certain minor incidents which are found in others, but the framework of the story is uninjured, and most of the Latin versions may be regarded as practically identical. In the library of the university of Cambridge there are two Latin versions, one Mm. IV, 6 (XIII[th] Cy.), the other Kk. II, 22 (XV[th]).

Even if it were possible to discover the precise manuscript from which the original of our O. F. text was taken, it would probably be impossible to establish the discovery by internal evidence afforded either by the Latin text or the derived version. The MSS. of the Cambridge Library have been to me the easiest of access, and I have chosen the MS. Mm. IV, 6 for comparison with the agn. text.

I may here add that no other Latin text which I have seen bears a closer resemblance to the agn. text. But, on the other hand, it is evident that the version of Mm. IV, 6 in its present form was not actually the source of our text. There are passages in our poem which point to another Latin version, and for which parallel passages are to be found in other Latin versions at our disposal. In v. 200 we

find the words "Cesse de ma persone", and in the MS. B. N.
17002 (and others) we read "Cessa de meä personnä". In
the description of the dragon (v. 168) we find the phrase
"russe barbe aveit", which corresponds to "barba eius aurea"
of B. N. 11705. Neither of these passages is in the Camb. MS.
Other discrepancies might be adduced, but a comparison of
the agn. version with the Latin version Mm. IV, 6 will
justify me in adopting the latter as being, practically, the
basis of the former. I subjoin a list of the most striking
resemblances.

The Cambridge MS. Mm. IV, 6 is a folio of 53 sheets
in double columns of 38 lines, and is dated XIII[th] Cy. Beside
the life of St. Margaret, it contains a Latin Life of St. Francis
(ff. 1—15), a Life of St. Dominic by "Frater Constantinus"
(15b—31) and a Life of St. Edmund (ff. 37—53). The Life
of St. Margaret ("Passio Sancte Margarete Virginis et Martyris") occupies ff. 31b—36. The writing is clear and distinct,
and the Latin style much better than that of many other
existing versions.

The MS. Kk. II, 22 is very illegible, and dates from late
in the XV[th] Century.

# Illustrative readings from the Latin Text.

(Camb.) Mm. IV, 6.

---

1. Post passionem et resurrectionem Domini nostri Jhesu Cristi, et gloriosam ascensionem eius in celo ad Deum patrem suum omnipotentem in illius nomine multi passi sunt martires, et coronati sunt apud Deum &c.
20. Margareta erat Theodosii filia, qui erat gentilium patriarcha et idola adorabat &c.
36. Mox autem ut nata est, ad nutriendam in quadam civitate ab Antiochiā stadia **quindecim** suscepta est.
39. A sua nutrice diligenter nutriebatur.
46. Ampliori desiderio tenebatur a sua nutrice.
47. Odiosa erat patri suo.
52. Audivit omnia certamina martirum et effusionem sanguinis iustorum in illis temporibus.
57. Erat namque annorum quindecim.
58. Pascebat oves nutricis sue, cum ceteris puellis suis coetaneis.
62. Si libera est accipiam eam ad uxorem, si ancilla est dabo pretium pro eā &c.
77. Jussit eam venire ad se.
88. Ne perdas cum impiis animam meam.
89. Video enim me sicut ovem in medio luporum.
93. Quomodo nuncuparis? Quem deum colis vel adoras?
95. Libera sum et cristiana. Nomen meum Margareta est. Ego invoco Deum omnipotentem et filium eius.
97 &c. Quem patres tui crucifixerunt, et ideo perierunt.

101 &c. Tunc iratus prefectus iussit M. in carcere concludi donec inveniret per qualem machinationem virginitatem eius perderet.

105. Introivit vero iniquus prefectus in Antiochiam civitatem, et adorabat deos surdos et mutos.

108. iussit adducere puellam.

109. et dixit ad eam. O puella miserere corporis tui &c.

110. adora deos meos.

111. multam dabo tibi pecuniam.

112. Et si obedieris mi et adoraveris deos meos, copulaverim te mi in amorem, accipiam te in coniugem, et erit tibi bene sicut et mi.

113 &c. M. respondit. Cognoscat Deus qui virginitatem meam consignavit, quod me suadere non debes, nec poteris me movere de viā veritatis per quam ego ambulare inchoavi. Nam illum adoro quem terra contremiscit, mare formidat, quem timet omnis creatura; cuius regnum permanet in secula seculorum.

121. Ego tradam corpus meum Deo meo J. C. ut cum iustis virginibus ab eo coronam accipiam. Christus se met ipsum pro nobis tradidit in mortem, et ego pro ipso mori non dubito.

125. iussit eam in aerem suspendi et virgis cedi.

129. in te, domine, speravi.

130 &c. sed mitte rorem de celo, ut mitigentur plage meę et dolor requiescat.

135. Ipsa orabat, et questionarius cedebat virgis tenerum corpus, et sanguis eius tanquam acqua de fonte purissimo decurrebat in terram.

141 &c. Nam pro multa effusione sanguinis illic assistentes omnes flebant super eam amarissime ... Ipse prefectus iracundus est tibi et perdere te festinat et delere memoriam tuam.

146. O mali consiliarii, ite ad opera vestra: mi autem Deus meus adiutor est.

4

152 &c. Carnifices vero accesserunt et mactaverunt corpus
eius. Impius prefectus clamide operiebat faciem suam,
quia propter effusionem sanguinis non poterat aspicere
in eam. Similiter et ceteri faciebant.

157. Si non adoraveris deos meos, gladius meus dominabitur
carni tuę, et ossa tua disperdam super ignem ardentem.

160 &c. O impudice et audax — si in carne mea data est
tibi potestas, animam autem meam eruet Christus de
manu tuā.

165. Consignavit corpus suum signaculo Christi.

166 &c. Ecce subito de angulo carceris exibat draco horribilis
cuius dentes erant ut ferrum acutum, oculi eius ut flamma
ignis splendebant, et de naribus eius ignis et fumus
exibat . . . et gladius ex utracque parte acutus videbatur.

174. Factum est lumen in carcere ab igne qui exibat de ore
draconis.

178. miserere mei quia sola orphana sum.

179. ne permittas hanc feram nocere mi.

181. et deglutivit in ventrem suam.

182 &c. Sed crucem Christi sibi fecit beata M. in ore draconis
et in duas partes eum divisit . . . Exivit de intero draconis
nullum dolorem in se habens.

186. vidit alium diabolum sedentem ut hominem nigrum,
habentem manus suas ad genua colligatas.

193. cepit ambulare ad eum, et tenuit manum eius.

194. Comprehendens demonem per capellos delisit eum in
terram, et posuit pedem suum super cervicem suam.

200. Cessa iam maligne de mea virginitate.

202. ego ancilla Christi, ego sposa Dei.

210. aperiam tibi portas paradisi.

212. gracias agens Deo, M. conversa ad demonem dixit . . .

215. alleva pedem tuum de cervice mea . . . et enarrabo tibi
omnia opera mea.

218. Tunc sancta puella elevavit calcaneum suum de cervice
eius.

220. post Belzebub princeps fui.

223. Contra omnem iusticiam pugnavi, et multorum iustorum laborem extinxi...

225 &c. Et qui tibi sunt similes, confusus et vacuus ab eis discedo, quemadmodum a te hodie.

227. Arma mea confracta sunt. Ego video Christum in te manentem. Nunc facis de me quod tibi placet. A tenera puellā superatus sum.

231 &c. Sed mi magis dolet quod pater tuus et mater tua socii̇ mei fuerunt et tu adversum me pugnasti, meque superasti.

235 &c. quis vobis precepit sanctis operibus adversari?

240. Unde est vita tua, vel quomodo in te Christus ingressus est? Dic mi unde fides tua, et ego dicam tibi omnia opera mea.

242. Michi non licet hęc nunciare tibi quia dignus non es audire vocem meam. Gracia Dei sum id quod sum.

245. Sathanas rex noster est, qui proiectus est de paradiso.

252. Rufonem fratrem meum occidisti.

253. Ego autem non sum ausus magis loqui tibi.

254. Quia video Christum circa te ambulantem.

255. Sed peto a te ancilla Christi, relaxa me modicum.

257. Ne amplius dampnes me, sed liga me in manu terrę...

261. terra eum statim deglutivit.

268. Cum exiret de carcere consignavit se signaculo Christi.

269. Tunc venerunt cuncti de ipsa civitate, ut viderent quę patiebatur.

272. Consenti mi et adora deos meos.

274. Te decet adorare Deum meum et J. C. filium eius... et non esse amicum idolorum mutorum.

276. Tunc iussit eam exspoliari, et in aerem suspendi, et cum lampadibus ardentibus accendi &c.

285. Ure cor meum, ut in me non sit iniquitas.

287. Consenti mi et sacrifica diis meis.

289. Non consentio nec adoro deos tuos surdos et mutos.

291. iussit afferri vas magnum, et impleri acquā et ligari manus, et in eam mitti, et ibi mortificari.

4*

296. Domine qui regnas in eternum.
302. Columba venit de celo et sedit super Margaretam.
305. Tunc solutę sunt manus eius et pedes et exivit de acqua
laudans et benedicens Deum &c.
312. Veni, M, in requiem Christi, Veni in regnum celorum,
Beata es qui coronam vitę accepisti, quia virginitatem
desiderasti.
316. In ipsa hora crediderunt in J. C. mille, exceptis mulieri-
bus et puellis.
319. iussit eos decollari et decollati sunt.
320. Et post paululum iussit Margaretam gladio interfici.
Statimque comprehenderunt eam questionarii et duxerunt
eam foras civitatem.
325. Et dixit ad eam unus ex illis, nomine Malcus, Extende
cervicem tuam et suscipe gladium meum.
328. Quia video circa te Christum stantem cum suis angelis.
330. peto frater ut si Christum vides, ut parcas mi usquedum
orationem meam finiam et commendo animam meam
domino J. C.
336. Deus qui celum mensurasti, et terrę fundamentum posu-
isti, exaudi deprecationem meam, et presta ut si quis
legerit librum gesti mei, vel audierit legere passionem
meam, ut ex illa hora deleatur peccatum eius. Et qui
cum suo lumine venerit ad ecclesiam ubi sunt reliquię
meę, in illa hora dimittantur peccata illius. Adhuc peto
domine, ut qui ecclesiam in nomine meo fecerit, aut quis
librum passionis meę scripserit, vel qui cum suo precio
illum emerit, reple illum de spiritu sancto, domine, et
in domo illius non nascatur infans claudus aut cecus aut
mutus neque a spiritu immundo temptatus, et si veniam
de peccato suo petierit, Domine digneris ei dimittere.
355. Factus est tonitruus magnus et columba venit de celo...
361. Beata es ... ubi sunt reliquię tuę ... spiritus nequitiae
non ingredietur.
368. Benedicebat Deum, dicens ...
369. Frater tolle gladium tuum et percute me.

370. Non faciam ... audivi tecum Christum loquentem.

371. Si hoc non feceris non habebis partem mecum in paradiso Dei.

372. Tunc percussor cum tremore nimis attulit gladium suum et amputavit caput eius.

375. Tunc venerunt angeli laudantes Deum, et sederunt super corpus beatę M. Venientes quoque demones, vociferabant dicentes, Unus Deus fortis, unus Deus magnus, unus Deus omnipotens.

378. Ego ... Theotinus tuli reliquias ... et posui eas ... in scrineum lapideum. Ego orationes eius scribebam et transmisi omnibus in Christo credentibus.

384. Angeli vero tollentes animam eius ascenderunt super nubem et deferebant eam in excelso, laudantes Deum &c.

388. Audientes autem hęc omnes infirmi ceci et claudi, surdi et muti, et a demone vexati veniebant ad corpus M et salvi fiebant.

Frederic Spencer, son of Rev. Joseph Spencer and Harriet Edgcome (née Blamey) his wife, was born at Newbury, England on the 29ᵗʰ September 1861. Educated at New Kingswood School, Bath from 1871 to 1878, in which year he matriculated in the University of London. Passed the intermediate examination (Arts) in 1879, and was granted the degree of Bachelor of Arts in 1881. Read Classics for two sessions in the Academy of Paris (École des Hautes Études) under the guidance of MM. Benoist, Havet, Tournier, and Weill (1882—1883). Entered the University of Cambridge in Oct. 1883 and read mathematics for one year. For two years (1884—1886) read Romance Languages under the direction of Dr. Eugen Braunholtz, university lecturer, and was awarded an honours degree in this branch of study in June 1886. In June 1887 appointed Master in Modern Languages at the Leys School Cambridge, and entered upon the duties of this post in September 1887.

www.ingramcontent.com/pod-product-compliance
Lightning Source LLC
Chambersburg PA
CBHW022201020726
47496CB00008B/2827